The Fabulous Fish from Lake Wiggawalla

BY TEDDY SLATER
PICTURES BY LAURA RANKIN

Silver Press

For Fabulous Fred Margulies.
—T.S.

This is for Floyd and Goldie, with love.
—L.R.

Library of Congress Cataloging-in-Publication Data
Slater, Teddy.
    The fabulous fish from Lake Wiggawalla / by Teddy Slater;
pictures by Laura Rankin.
        p. cm.—(Is that so?)
    Summary: Eleanor the exaggerator gets a bit boastful in
describing her summer vacation to the other students. At
intervals readers are given a variety of similar boasts from
which to choose.
    [1. Vacations—Fiction. 2. Literary recreations.]
I. Rankin, Laura, ill. II. Title. III. Series: Slater, Teddy.
Is that so?
PZ7.S6294Fab   1991
[E]—dc20   90-38178
ISBN 0-671-70409-5 (LSB)   ISBN 0-671-70413-3   CIP
                                                   AC

Produced by Small Packages, Inc.
Text copyright © 1991 Small Packages, Inc.
and Teddy Slater

Illustrations copyright © 1991 Small Packages, Inc.
and Laura Rankin.

Published by Silver Press, a division of
Silver Burdett Press, Inc.
Simon & Schuster, Inc.
Prentice Hall Bldg., Englewood Cliffs, NJ 07632.

Printed in the United States of America.

10 9 8 7 6 5 4 3 2 1

On the first day of school, Miss Pennywhistle said, "Who would
like to tell the class about his or her summer vacation?"
"Me! Me!" cried Eleanor the exaggerator. "My family and I
had the best vacation ever."
"Go ahead, Eleanor," Miss Pennywhistle said.

"We started out here in Pennsylvania," Eleanor said.
"And we drove all the way to China."
"Is that so?" yelled noisy Nellie.
Eleanor shrugged. "Well. . .maybe I did exaggerate a little bit."

How far do you think Eleanor and her family really drove?

Did they drive as far as
the moon and back?

Did they drive as far as
the attic?

Did they drive as far as
the North Pole?

Or did they drive
as far as Maine?

"It's true we only drove to Maine," Eleanor admitted.
"But we couldn't have picked a better place for a vacation.
My grandma and grandpa have a great big log cabin there,
right on the shore of Lake Wiggawalla.

"Lake Wiggawalla is full of fish," Eleanor continued.
"There must be a million of them! So every morning
we took our fishing rods and rowed out to catch some.

"One day I caught the most fabulous fish ever. It was as big as
a whale—and twice as strong! That's why it got away."
"Is that so?" asked Danny the doubter.
Eleanor smiled. "Well. . .maybe I did exaggerate a wee bit."

How strong do you think Eleanor's fish really was?

Was it strong enough
to tow two waterskiers
across the lake,

strong enough to lift
a 100-pound barbell
with its flippers,

strong enough to snap the
fishing line and swim away,

or strong enough to carry
a whole troop of Girl Scouts
on its back?

"It's true my fish just managed to break the line," Eleanor said.
"But I was glad it swam away. I really don't care much for fish.
I'd much rather eat blueberries!

"I bet there are a billion blueberries on the bushes by
Lake Wiggawalla," Eleanor went on. "So every afternoon
we went out berry picking.

"Mommy and Daddy weren't very good pickers. In fact, they always ate more than they brought back with them. But I needed a great big wheelbarrow to carry home all the berries *I* picked."

"Is that so?" asked Scott the scoffer.

Eleanor grinned. "Well. . . maybe I did exaggerate a teeny-weeny bit."

How many blueberries do you think Eleanor really picked?

Did she pick far too many
to fit in a closet?

Did she pick a few too many
to fit in a teaspoon?

Did she pick almost enough
to fill a swimming pool?

Or did she pick just enough
to fill two small buckets?

"It's true I only filled two buckets a day," Eleanor admitted.
"But Grandma made the most of every berry. She made blueberry
pies and blueberry muffins, and blueberry waffles with
blueberry jam. She even made blueberry bread and the very
berriest blueberry ice cream!

"But it was Grandpa who made the best thing of all,"
Eleanor went on. "Day after day, he hammered and sawed.
Then he sanded and painted. And finally it was finished. . .

" . . . the most wonderful treehouse ever. It looked a lot like
Grandma and Grandpa's cabin, but it was ten times as big!"
"Is that so?" asked curious Caroline.
Eleanor giggled. "Well . . . maybe I did exaggerate an itsy-bitsy bit."

How big do you think Eleanor's treehouse really was?

Was it a little bigger than
Grandma's four-poster bed,

a little smaller than
Eleanor's five-room dollhouse,

almost as big as
a skyscraper,

or just about the size of
the Wiggawalla ferryboat?

"It's true my treehouse wasn't much bigger than Grandma's bed,"
Eleanor admitted. "But it was exactly the right size for me.
On hot summer days there was no better place to catch a breeze.

"And on cool summer nights there was no better place to
cuddle up and count the stars. There must have been
a trillion of them, all shining down on Lake Wiggawalla."

"Is that so?" asked Norman the know-it-all.
Eleanor laughed. "Well...maybe I did exaggerate
an itsy-bitsy, teeny-weeny, wee little bit."
"No, Eleanor," Miss Pennywhistle said. "This time
I don't think you did!" And the teacher laughed, too.